THE BEAST AND THE BOY

The Beast and the Boy

By Massimo Mostacchi
Illustrated by Monica Miceli
English adaptation by Andrew Clements

A MICHAEL NEUGEBUAER BOOK
NORTH-SOUTH BOOKS / NEW YORK / LONDON

There once was a beast, and the forest was his home.
All his life other animals had run and hidden when he
wanted to play. And he didn't know why.
Beasts don't have mirrors, so he'd never looked at himself.
All he knew about himself were his own thoughts, which
were kind and good and friendly.
He didn't know that he had sharp eyes and long fangs
and a mane like a lion.
So the beast had always lived alone in the forest.

One afternoon the beast left the forest and went into the town.
Some children were playing, and he wanted to join in their game.
But they did not see a friend coming. They saw a beast.

"Help! Help! It's a horrible beast!" The children ran away screaming.

With tears running down his face, the beast went back to the forest.
"I guess that's what I am—a horrible beast. And if that's what I am,"
he snarled, "then that's how I'm going to act!"

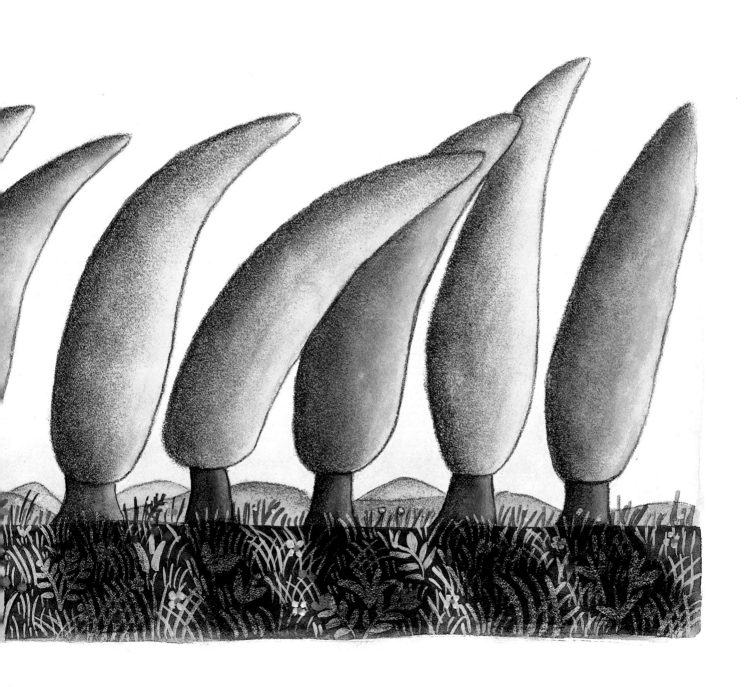

Just then he heard footsteps, and he crouched behind a tree.

"Aha!" thought the beast. "An animal, or maybe a fierce hunter—I'm going to pounce and bite!"

But it was only a little boy. And when the boy saw the beast, he didn't scream and he didn't run away. He just said "Hello" and smiled.

The beast was so surprised, he said "Hello" right back.

"What are you doing alone in the forest? Don't you know there are wild beasts here?"

The boy said, "I don't care. Everyone thinks I'm weak and small, but I'm not afraid of anything. All the children are mean to me. I haven't got a single friend. So I've run away from home."

"No one is nice to me, either," said the beast. "Maybe we could be friends."

The beast and the boy romped and laughed in the twilight.
They played hide-and-seek in the leaves, and they wrestled and ran and
tumbled and laughed until they were all worn out.
Then the beast and the boy curled up together and went to sleep.

When the boy's parents came home from work, they could not find him.
Then his father saw a note on the boy's pillow. It said, "I've gone away to find
a friend. Please don't worry about me. Love. Marco."

His mother and father raced off to find him.

They walked deep into the woods. But soon it got very dark, and through the shadowy forest they heard a long, hungry howling—*aaahhOOooooooooooooo.* Wolves! Marco's parents built a fire, and just in time.

A pack of wolves surrounded them, and only the flickering firelight
kept them away. But the fire burned lower and lower, and when it had
almost gone out, Marco's mother screamed at the top of her voice,
"HELP! HELLLLLP!"

Marco woke up instantly and shook the beast.
"That's my mother calling for help. Let's go!"

Marco leaped onto the beast's back and they dashed through the woods.

With a roar and a yell, the beast and the boy charged into the clearing.
The wolves took one look, then turned tail and ran away, with the
beast snapping at their heels.

Marco ran to his mother and father. "You've saved us, Marco!
I'm so proud of you," said his father.

"Now," said his mother, "let's go home."

But Marco said, "We can't leave until my friend gets back—and here
he comes!"

When Marco's parents saw the beast running towards them, they jumped behind a tree. But the beast stopped and sat down. Marco patted him on the head. "This is my new friend. You don't have to be afraid. He just looks scary," said Marco.

"Now we can all go home."

And that's what they did.

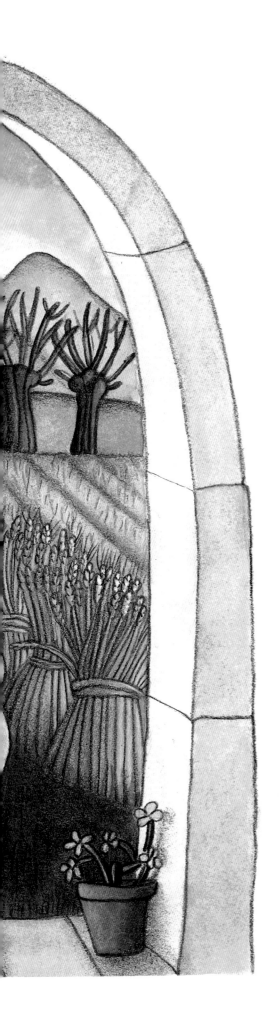

By the next afternoon, everyone in town had heard how
Marco's parents had been saved from a pack of hungry wolves.
All the children were invited to Marco's house for a celebration.

When they came. they did not see a weak little boy.
and they did not see a big scary beast.

All they saw were two good friends.

Copyright © 1995 by Michael Neugebauer Verlag AG
First published in Switzerland under the title *Marcolino und das Monster*
by Michael Neugebauer Verlag AG. Gossau Zürich. Switzerland.

Published in the United States. Canada. Great Britain. Australia. and New Zealand in 1995
by North-South Books. an imprint of Nord-Süd Verlag AG. Gossau Zürich. Switzerland.

Distributed in the United States by North-South Books Inc.. New York

Library of Congress Cataloging-in-Publication Data is available
A CIP catalogue record for this book is available from The British Library
ISBN 1-55858-443-9 (TRADE BINDING) 10 9 8 7 6 5 4 3 2 1
ISBN 1-55858-444-7 (LIBRARY BINDING) 10 9 8 7 6 5 4 3 2 1
Printed in Belgium